A Sled Dog Morning

Written by
Laura Appleton-Smith

Illustrated by
Keinyo White

Laura Appleton-Smith was born and raised in Vermont and holds a degree in English from Middlebury College. Laura is a primary schoolteacher who has combined her talents in creative writing and her experience in early childhood education to create *Books to Remember*. Laura lives in New Hampshire with her husband, Terry.

Keinyo White is a graduate of the Rhode Island School of Design with a B.F.A. in illustration. He currently produces children's books and freelance illustrations from his studio in Los Angeles. This is his fourth book for Flyleaf Publishing.

A Book to Remember™
Published by Flyleaf Publishing
Post Office Box 287, Lyme, NH 03768

For orders or information, contact us at **(800) 449-7006**.
Please visit our website at **www.flyleafpublishing.com**

First Edition
Library of Congress Catalog Card Number: 2002117646
Hard cover ISBN-13: 978-1-929262-17-5
Hard cover ISBN-10: 1-929262-17-5
Soft cover ISBN-13: 978-1-929262-18-2
Soft cover ISBN-10: 1-929262-18-3

For Keinyo.
Thank you for sharing your artistic talent with us over the years,
and thank you especially for your work on this book.
We should celebrate over a latte...

LAS

—

For Kari and Ajani;
and for Anisa for being the best model I have ever worked with.

KW

It is morning but the sun is not up yet.
Mom rests her hand on my back.

"Sedna, the pups were born," she informs me.

I jump from bed and pull on pants and a jacket.

I get dressed so fast I put my mukluks on backwards, but I cannot stop to fix them.

I run past my Dad and my big stack of flapjacks.
"Can't you stop for corn flapjacks, Sedna?"
Dad asks as he hands me a fork.

"Forget the flapjacks, the pups were born!"
I yell as I run out the door.

The dog kennel stores the dog sleds,
as well as the pens for the sled dogs.

The dogs snack on their morning kibble as I pass.

A big box is in the back corner of the kennel.

In the box, amidst the torn blankets,

I spot our Alaskan Sled Dog Storm and her six pups.

Storm licks a black pup.

The rest of the pups drink Storm's milk.

Mom and Dad enter the kennel.
Mom tells me to sit on the floor.

She lifts the black pup from the box
and helps me to support him with my hands.

The pup is so soft. He grunts and licks my neck.

"He must want milk," I tell Mom.
She helps me put him back in the box.

Dad is putting the sled dogs into dog boxes
in the back of his Ford pickup truck.

Sled dog running is Dad's sport,
and there is a contest this morning.

We put the sled on top of the truck and set off.

At the contest we snap the dogs
onto the cord that pulls the sled.

We snap in Orbit and then Rocket,
Red Hot and then Bandit,
and at last Lord Tom and Baron.

I help Dad escort the dogs to the track.

The dogs are set to run.
They jump and yelp until a horn blasts.

The dogs sprint off.

Dad kicks the sled forward to help the dogs run faster.

It is a brisk morning and the sled is quick on the track.
There is frost in the forest.

The dogs run well. They are strong pulling the sled.

Dad's sled is the fastest in the contest!

We win a ribbon.

On the trip back Dad tells me,
"Sedna, I am glad to win the contest,
but the best thing for me is to be out in the forest
with you and the dogs on a brisk morning."

I am glad.

Back at the kennel I run in to visit the pups.
They will be fast sled dogs when they get big.

Perhaps I will run them when I am big, just like my Dad.

A Sled Dog Morning is decodable with the knowledge of the 26 phonetic alphabet sounds, plus the "or" phonogram, and the ability to blend those sounds together.

Puzzle Words are words used in the story that are either irregular or have sound/spelling correspondences that the reader may not be familiar with.

The **Puzzle Word Review List** contains Puzzle Words that have been introduced in previous books in the *Books to Remember* Series.

Please Note: If all of the words on this page are pre-taught and the reader knows the 26 phonetic alphabet sounds, plus the phonogram listed above, and has the ability to blend those sounds together, this book is 100% phonetically decodable.

Puzzle Words	Puzzle Word Review List		"or" Words	"er" Words
backwards	a	so	born	corner
door	are	that	cord	enter
floor	as	the	corn	faster
forward	be	their	corner	perhaps
kibble	he	them	door	
like	her	then	escort	
me	I	there	floor	
perhaps	into	they	for	
pull	is	thing	Ford	
pulling	my	this	forest	
stores	of	to	forget	
	onto	visit	fork	
	our	want	forward	
	out	we	horn	
	put	were	informs	
	putting	when	lord	
	she	with	morning	
		you	orbit	
			sport	
			stores	
			storm	
			support	
			torn	